Jon Scieszka's TRUCKTOWN
on Reading Street

ROSIE

PEARSON

Glenview, Illinois • Boston, Massachusetts • Chandler, Arizona
Shoreview, Minnesota • Upper Saddle River, New Jersey

We tap the building.

We pat the building.

I am Rosie. My building!

We like Rosie.

BAN

Rosie is big!

We like Rosie!